Big Bird Brings Spring to Sesame Street

By Lauren Collier Swindler
Illustrated by Marsha Winborn

This educational book was created in cooperation with the Children's Television Workshop, producers of Sesame Street. Children do not have to watch the television show to benefit from this book. Workshop revenues from this product will be used to help support CTW educational projects.

A SESAME STREET/GOLDEN PRESS BOOK
Published by Western Publishing Company, Inc. in conjunction with Children's Television Workshop.

MCMXCI

BIG BIRD looked down Sesame Street. Everything was
covered with a thick layer of white snow. Big Bird sighed.
It had been a long winter. He was tired of looking at plain
white snow.

Big Bird walked through the park and thought about all the things he couldn't do because of the snow. He couldn't ride his unicycle down Sesame Street. He couldn't play in the sandbox in the playground. He couldn't roller-skate on the sidewalk.

"Besides, winter is so gloomy," thought Big Bird.
"I wish spring were here." Suddenly Big Bird had a
wonderful idea. "I'll buy some flowers to put in my nest.
Then it will look like spring is already here."

So Big Bird walked down to Mr. MacIntosh's store and bought six of his favorite flowers.

"I feel better already," thought Big Bird as he walked
back toward Sesame Street with his bouquet of six
beautiful flowers.

On the way to his nest, Big Bird stopped at the Count's
castle.

"Ah, Big Bird, what beautiful flowers!" cried the Count.
"Let me count them. One beautiful flower, two beautiful
flowers, three, four, five, six beautiful flowers!

"Big Bird, I love counting your beautiful flowers."

"Gee, I didn't buy the flowers to count them," said Big Bird. "I bought them to remind me of spring. Would you like to keep this pretty pink daisy? You can count all of its petals."

"Wonderful!" cried the Count. "I also love counting flower petals. One pretty pink flower petal, two pretty pink flower petals, three..."

Big Bird walked down Sesame Street, carrying his five flowers. He stopped to watch Maria shovel snow from the sidewalk in front of the Fix-it Shop.

Oops! Maria slipped and fell in the snow.

"Oh, Maria, are you hurt?" asked Big Bird as he helped
her stand up.

"No, Big Bird, I'm not hurt. But I am tired of winter
and shoveling snow," she said.

"Here, Maria," said Big Bird. "You may have one of my flowers. It will help you feel happy again."

"Thank you, Big Bird," said Maria, taking the orange tiger lily.

Big Bird walked on down Sesame Street with the four
flowers he had left. He found Grover sitting sadly on
the steps.

"Oh, my goodness," said Grover unhappily. "Furry old
Grover is very blue."

"Of course you are blue," said Big Bird. "You have
blue fur."

"No, no, Big Bird. I mean that I am very sad,"
explained Grover. "I cannot ride my scooter in the snow."

"Maybe this blue pansy will make you feel better," said
Big Bird, and he gave it to Grover.

Big Bird looked down at his three flowers, and he
noticed that one of them was bent over. "Uh-oh," said Big
Bird, holding up the purple iris. "This flower's stem is broken."
The lid of the trash can clanged open. "I love things that
are broken!" said Oscar-the-Grouch, leaning out of his can.
"Well, gee, Oscar, I guess you may have my purple iris."

"Thanks, Bird," said Oscar. "Grouches like flowers that
are bent and broken. Heh, heh, heh." He grabbed the
purple iris and slammed down the lid of the trash can.

Big Bird clutched his last two flowers. Then he saw Ernie.

"Hi, Big Bird," said Ernie. "You look cold."

"I'm so cold my tail feathers are frozen," answered Big Bird. "Where are you going?"

"I'm going to see Betty Lou. She's sick in bed with the flu. I wish I had something to take her to cheer her up...."

"Oh," said Big Bird, looking down at his last two
flowers. "Do you think she would like a yellow daffodil?"
"Oh, yes! Thank you, Big Bird." Ernie took the flower
and went into 123 Sesame Street.

Big Bird went into Hooper's Store to get warm. Bert was sitting at the counter, sadly sipping his Figgy Fizz.

"What's wrong, Bert?" asked Big Bird. "You look kind of glum."

"I've lost my favorite paper clip," wailed Bert. "I dropped it in a snowdrift. Now I'll have to wait until the snow melts to find it. Oh, Big Bird, what if my paper clip gets all rusted by then?"

"Don't worry, Bert," said Big Bird. "Your paper clip will still be there in the spring."

"Ohhhhh, Big Bird!" sighed Bert. Then he looked at the single rose Big Bird was holding. "Say, what are you going to do with that beautiful rose?" he asked.

"Uh, er...I'm going to give it to you, Bert." Big Bird gave Bert his last flower, and left Hooper's Store.

Empty-handed, Big Bird walked back up Sesame Street toward his nest. He had given away all six of his flowers. "Oh, well," he thought. "Soon it will be spring."

When he got to the lamppost, Big Bird turned around.
Sesame Street looked different! The plain, white,
snow-covered street was splashed with bright colors. The
flowers Big Bird had given to his friends were blooming
up and down Sesame Street.
Big Bird had brought spring to Sesame Street.